Saint Clare of Assisi
Runaway Rich Girl

Saint Clare of Assisi
Runaway Rich Girl

Written and illustrated by
Kim Hee-ju

Pauline
BOOKS & MEDIA
Boston

Library of Congress Control Number: 2016958828
CIP data is available.

ISBN 10: 0-8198-9087-1
ISBN 13: 978-0-8198-9087-0

향기롭게 빛나는 클라라 (Shining Sweetly Clare) by KIM Hee-ju

© 2014 by KIM Hee-ju, www.pauline.or.kr.

Originally published by Pauline Books & Media, Seoul, Korea. All rights reserved.

Translated by Kyung Hee Yoon

Scripture quotations contained herein are from the *New Revised Standard Version Bible: Catholic Edition*, copyright © 1989, 1993, Division of Christian Education of the National Council of the Churches of Christ in the United States of America. Used by permission. All rights reserved.

Published by Pauline Books & Media, 50 Saint Paul's Avenue, Boston, MA 02130-3491

Printed in the U.S.A.

SCOA VSAUSAPEOILL12-1210079 9087-1

www.pauline.org

Pauline Books & Media is the publishing house of the Daughters of St. Paul, an international congregation of women religious serving the Church with the communications media.

1 2 3 4 5 6 7 8 9   21 20 19 18 17

LADY OF ASSISI

THE YEAR 1207

IN THE QUIET TOWN OF ASSISI IN THE UMBRIA REGION OF ITALY

LOOK! THAT'S FRANCIS BERNARDONE OVER THERE.

HE USED TO BE DRESSED IN FINE CLOTHES. NOW HE LOOKS LIKE A BEGGAR!

STOP

SLAM!

THAT RASCAL BERNARDONE!

POUND

POUND

HOW DARE BERNARDONE TELL ME HE'S GOING TO BUILD AN AREA IN TOWN FOR THE MERCHANTS!

PLEASE RELAX, BROTHER.

HE MUST THINK I'M A PUSHOVER, MONALDO! I AM THE NOBLEMAN HERE, NOT HIM.

LISTEN,

DON'T WORRY, BROTHER. THIS CLOTH MERCHANT WILL NOT TELL THE NOBLE OFFREDUCCIO FAMILY WHAT TO DO!

IN THE BEGINNING OF THE THIRTEENTH CENTURY, THE WORKING PEOPLE OF ASSISI AND MANY OTHER ITALIAN TOWNS FOUGHT TO GAIN MORE FREEDOM FROM THE RICH NOBLES. IN 1202, THE PEOPLE OF ASSISI TRIED TO TAKE OVER THE CITY. CIVIL WAR BROKE OUT. THE NOBLES SOUGHT ASSISTANCE FROM THE NEARBY CITY OF PERUGIA.

DURING THE WAR,
CLARE'S FAMILY FLED TO PERUGIA.

WITH PERUGIA'S HELP, THE NOBLES OF ASSISI WERE ABLE TO REGAIN CONTROL OF THEIR CITY. THE OFFREDUCCIOS RETURNED TO ASSISI IN 1205, WHEN CLARE WAS ELEVEN YEARS OLD.

1211, ASSISI

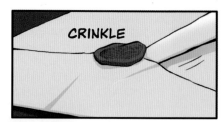

CRINKLE

HMM . . .

HE WANTS TO MARRY CLARE?

THIS MARRIAGE WOULD DEFINITELY BE TO OUR FAMILY'S BENEFIT.

* BONA DI GUELFUCCIO WAS CLARE'S RELATIVE AND FREQUENT COMPANION.

CLARE . . .

THERE YOU ARE!

WHY ARE YOU IN A GOOD MOOD, CATERINA*?

YOU HAVE A SPECIAL GUEST.

A GUEST?

YES. FATHER ASKED THAT I FIND YOU.

WHO IS IT?

* CATERINA, ONE OF CLARE'S YOUNGER SISTERS, FOLLOWED CLARE INTO RELIGIOUS LIFE AND BECAME SISTER AGNES.

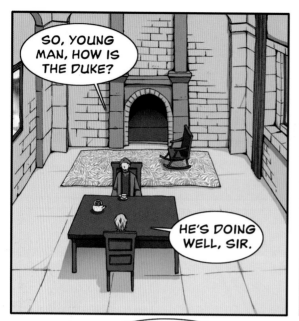

SOME TIME LATER

AH!

CLARE, DO YOU REMEMBER FRANCIS BERNARDONE?

OF COURSE. WHY?

HE'S JUST RETURNED FROM BEING AWAY FOR TWO YEARS.

REALLY?

YES, I HEARD HE WENT TO ROME TO ASK THE POPE'S PERMISSION TO BEGIN A RELIGIOUS ORDER.

DID HE RECEIVE IT?

I THINK SO. HE HAS A *TONSURE NOW AND HE IS OFTEN WITH BISHOP GUIDO.

*TONSURE: THE PRACTICE OF SHAVING SOME OR ALL OF THE HAIR ON THE SCALP, AS A SIGN OF RELIGIOUS DEVOTION OR HUMILITY.

HE BECAME A PRIEST?

I DON'T THINK SO.

I DON'T SEE HOW ANYONE CAN BADMOUTH HIM ANYMORE. HE HAS THE POPE'S APPROVAL TO CONTINUE TO DO AS HE HAS BEEN DOING.

REALLY?

OH . . . I SEE.

STILL, I THOUGHT HE WOULD BECOME A GREAT KNIGHT. I DON'T UNDERSTAND WHY FRANCIS GAVE UP EVERYTHING TO LIVE LIKE A BEGGAR AND FOLLOW GOD.

HMM . . .

YOU'VE ALWAYS LIKED HIM, HAVEN'T YOU, CLARE?

I SUPPOSE THAT'S BETWEEN GOD AND FRANCIS.

WHAT? I SIMPLY ADMIRE HIM.

HELLO LADIES, WHAT ARE YOU TALKING ABOUT?

LORD RANIERI!

GOOD MORNING, LADY BONA!

PLEASE JOIN US!

MY DEAR BROTHERS AND SISTERS, I'M HERE TODAY TO SHARE WITH YOU HOW GOD SAVED ME.

YOU MAY HAVE HEARD THAT I USED TO ONLY CARE ABOUT HAVING FUN.

BUT GOD HELPED ME UNDERSTAND THAT HE WANTED MORE FROM ME.

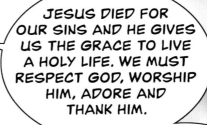

JESUS DIED FOR OUR SINS AND HE GIVES US THE GRACE TO LIVE A HOLY LIFE. WE MUST RESPECT GOD, WORSHIP HIM, ADORE AND THANK HIM.

ONE DAY WE ALL WILL FACE DEATH. WE NEED TO REPENT NOW AND TRY TO LIVE ACCORDING TO GOD'S WILL FOR US!

CONFESS YOUR SINS.
FORGIVE OTHERS AND GIVE GENEROUSLY
TO THE POOR. GOD LOVES US
AND HIS LOVE IS ALL WE REALLY NEED.

JESUS DIDN'T HAVE
FANCY CLOTHES OR LIVE IN A CASTLE.
HE WAS BORN IN A STABLE AND LIVED
A LIFE OF SIMPLE POVERTY.

ONCE JESUS TOLD ONE OF HIS
FOLLOWERS THAT BIRDS AND FOXES
HAVE PLACES TO SLEEP BUT HE—
THE SON OF GOD—

HAD NOWHERE TO LAY HIS HEAD!
A LIFE OF POVERTY,
RELYING COMPLETELY ON GOD
FOR EVERYTHING, IS A BLESSING!

....

CLARE?

CLARE!

ARE YOU OK?

!

I'VE BEEN CALLING YOUR NAME. . . .

WHAT? OH, SORRY.

I WAS JUST . . . THINKING. LET'S GO HOME.

RUSHES OFF

A FEW DAYS LATER

HI, CLARE, LONG TIME NO SEE!

RUFINO*! YOU JOINED BROTHER FRANCIS?

YES, AND I'VE NEVER BEEN HAPPIER.

WHERE ARE YOU GOING?

I'M HEADED TO THE PORZIUNCOLA CHAPEL WITH SOME BREAD THE BAKER HAS GIVEN US. FRANCIS AND THE OTHER BROTHERS ARE THERE.

*RUFINO DI SCIPIONE WAS CLARE'S COUSIN. HE WAS ALSO A FRIAR IN FRANCIS' ORDER.

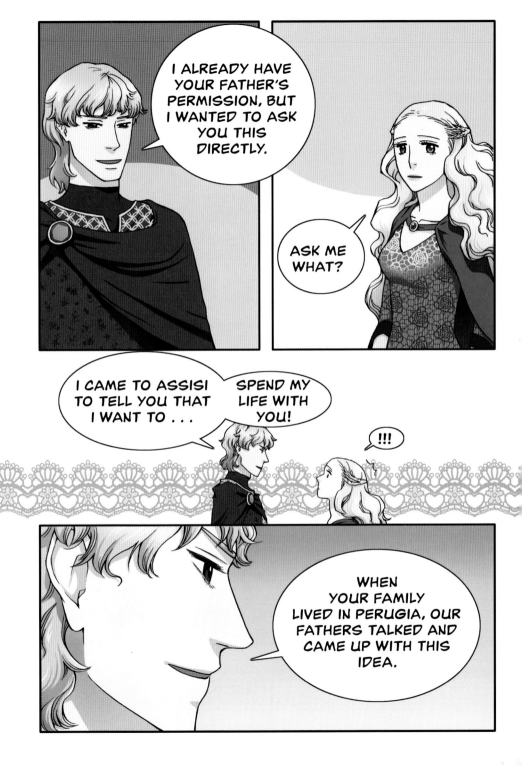

NO ONE SEEMS TO CARE WHAT I THINK. MOTHER AND FATHER ARE ALREADY PLANNING THE WEDDING!

PERHAPS THEY THINK THE MARRIAGE IS GOOD FOR THE FAMILY.

?

DO YOU LOVE RANIERI?

HE'S ALSO HANDSOME AND STRONG. I'M SURE HE'D BE A GOOD HUSBAND.

THEN WHY HESITATE?

HE'S VERY UNDERSTANDING AND SWEET.

BONA, I'M EIGHTEEN AND MOST GIRLS MY AGE ARE GETTING MARRIED OR ARE MARRIED ALREADY. BUT . . . I JUST DON'T KNOW.

. . .

SIGH . . .

DOES THIS HAVE ANYTHING TO DO WITH FRANCIS?!

BELONGING TO JESUS

AMADEO, FETCH!

SHALL WE EAT NOW?

THUMP

OOPS, I THREW IT TOO FAR!

I'LL GET IT, CATERINA.

MAYBE THE CHURCH HE'S BEEN FIXING IS AROUND HERE.

I SHOULD SAY HELLO . . .

HI—

!!!!!

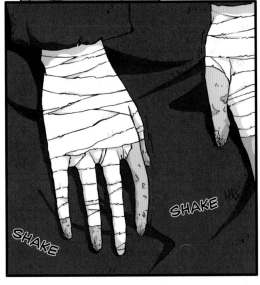

SHAKE

SHAKE

GASP!

!

THANK YOU!

THANK YOU SO MUCH!

THANK YOU SO VERY MUCH!

HOW?

SHAKE

HOW COULD HE . . .

. . . KISS THAT LEPER?

LADY CLARE?

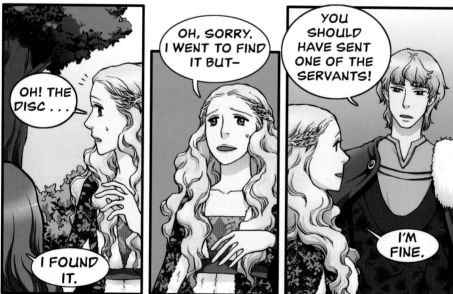

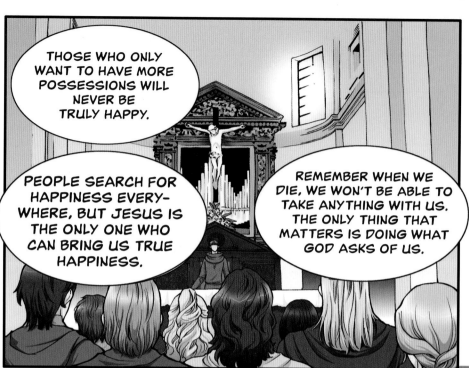

THOSE WHO ONLY WANT TO HAVE MORE POSSESSIONS WILL NEVER BE TRULY HAPPY.

PEOPLE SEARCH FOR HAPPINESS EVERYWHERE, BUT JESUS IS THE ONLY ONE WHO CAN BRING US TRUE HAPPINESS.

REMEMBER WHEN WE DIE, WE WON'T BE ABLE TO TAKE ANYTHING WITH US. THE ONLY THING THAT MATTERS IS DOING WHAT GOD ASKS OF US.

BROTHERS AND SISTERS, ASK YOURSELVES, HOW DOES GOD WANT YOU TO LIVE? HOW DOES GOD WANT YOU TO BE HAPPY?

BROTHER FRANCIS!

HESITATE

UMM . . .

CHATTER

LATELY, I'VE BECOME AWARE OF FEELING SO EMPTY.

WHAT SHOULD I DO?

THAT'S JUST A SIGN THAT YOU NEED TO SPEND MORE TIME IN PRAYER.

!

GOD WANTS TO FILL YOUR EMPTINESS, SO AVOID THE DARKNESS OF YOUR MIND AND PRAY. GOD WILL HELP YOU.

CAN I DISCUSS THESE THINGS WITH YOU AGAIN?

OF COURSE, LADY CLARE. ANYTIME.

WHERE IS LADY CLARE?

SHE WENT TO LISTEN TO BROTHER FRANCIS PREACH, SIR.

THAT'S WHAT YOU SAID YESTERDAY AND THE DAY BEFORE!

YES SIR, SHE GOES DAILY.

THAT WILL CHANGE WHEN WE'RE IN PERUGIA.

LEAVE. I WANT TO BE ALONE.

GRASP

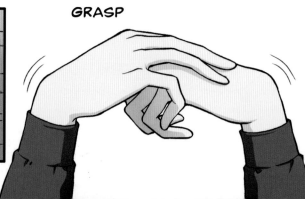

STOP

I FOUND YOU.

!

LORD RANIERI!

GIVING BREAD TO THOSE IN NEED? YOU HAVE SUCH A KIND HEART—LIKE AN ANGEL.

PLEASE, LORD RANIERI . . .

BLUSH

IT'S JUST . . .

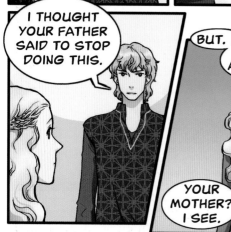

I THOUGHT YOUR FATHER SAID TO STOP DOING THIS.

BUT. . . MOTHER APPROVES.

YOUR MOTHER? I SEE.

LORD RANIERI, ARE YOU GOING TO TELL ME I'M WEIRD FOR DOING THIS?

NO, OF COURSE NOT. YOU'RE JUST SERVING THE POOR AS GOD TELLS US TO DO.

I DON'T THINK YOU'RE WEIRD.

IT'S JUST, YOU'RE SO BUSY. I NEVER GET TO SEE YOU.

WERE YOU LOOKING FOR ME?

OF COURSE, CLARE. YOU'RE TO BE MY BRIDE!

!

GASP

SIGH

GREAT SERMON, BROTHER FRANCIS.

LADY CLARE SEEMED VERY MOVED BY YOUR PREACHING.

IT'S TOO BAD THAT SHE'LL MOVE TO PERUGIA AFTER HER WEDDING.

NO, SHE WON'T.

WHAT DO YOU MEAN?

CLARE JUST TOLD ME THAT SHE HAS DECIDED TO GIVE HER LIFE TO GOD.

WHAT!
ARE YOU SURE!?

YES.

SHE IS GOING
TO GIVE UP EVERYTHING
AND FOLLOW JESUS
IN A LIFE
OF POVERTY.

I'M SHOCKED.
HER MARRIAGE
INTO A NOBLE FAMILY
IN PERUGIA HAS
ALREADY BEEN
ARRANGED!

I IMAGINE
HER FAMILY WILL
NOT BE HAPPY,
ESPECIALLY HER
FATHER.

LADY CLARE
IS QUITE
BRAVE IF
SHE PLANS
ON GOING
AGAINST HER
FATHER'S
WISHES!

NOD

MOTHER AND CATERINA, WHEN WILL I SEE YOU AGAIN?

LORD RANIERI, I WISH I DIDN'T HAVE TO BREAK YOUR HEART. YOU'RE A GOOD MAN, BUT I BELONG ONLY TO GOD.

I'M SO SORRY.

SOB

CLARE?!

GASP

I HOPE YOU UNDERSTAND SOME DAY.

CLARE, ARE YOU OKAY?

!

SISTER, WHAT'S WRONG?

ARGH! WHY AM I CRYING? I DON'T WANT THEM TO REMEMBER ME LIKE THIS.

WIPE

N-N-NOTHING IS WRONG.

. . .

I JUST FEEL EMOTIONAL.

ARE YOU REALLY OKAY?

CATERINA, I'M FINE.

IF BISHOP GUIDO GIVES ME THE PALM, IT IS A SIGN THAT I AM TO LEAVE TONIGHT.

THIS IS IT.

NOD

THANK
YOU FOR
THE PALM,
BISHOP
GUIDO!

I WONDER WHAT WOKE ME? MY HEART IS BEATING SO HARD . . .

RISING FROM HER BED AND LEAVING HER ROOM, LADY ORTOLANA—CLARE'S MOTHER—COULD HARDLY BELIEVE WHAT SHE SAW.

!

CLARE?

GASP

HUFF

PUFF

PANT

KNEEL

CLUNK

ONCE I GET TO THE OTHER SIDE OF THIS WALL, MY LIFE WILL CHANGE FOREVER.

AHA!

PANT PANT

TODAY LADY CLARE
THE NOBLEWOMAN
WILL DIE!

AND I WILL BE REBORN
AS SISTER CLARE,
A POOR LADY TOTALLY
DEDICATED TO GOD.

CLARE WENT TO THE CHAPEL OF THE PORZI-UNCULA WITH BONA TO MEET BROTHER FRANCIS AND HIS COMPANIONS.

BROTHER FRANCIS ACCEPTED
CLARE'S VOW TO EMBRACE A LIFE OF
POVERTY, CHASTITY, AND OBEDIENCE.

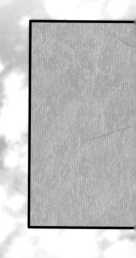

CLARE'S BEAUTIFUL, LONG HAIR WAS CUT TO SYMBOLIZE THAT SHE NO LONGER BELONGED TO THE WORLD.

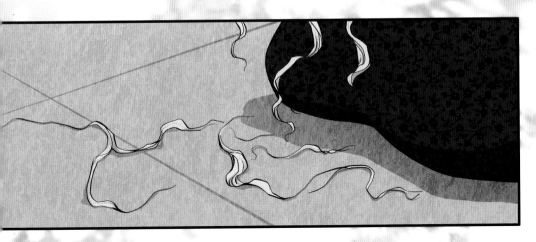

LADY CLARE IS NOWHERE TO BE FOUND THIS MORNING.

WE FOUND THAT SOMEONE HAD UNSEALED A STONE DOOR IN THE WALL THAT WE USUALLY KEEP SEALED.

BOTH LADY CLARE AND BONA ARE MISSING.

SHE MUST HAVE RUN AWAY LAST NIGHT . . .

ABSURD!

WHY WOULD SHE LEAVE ME?

CLENCH

WHERE DO YOU THINK SHE IS? TELL US!

FRANCIS, I'M SURE BROTHER FRANCIS KNOWS WHERE SHE IS.

I WILL NOT RETURN WITH YOU.

OH YES YOU WILL. YOU'RE COMING HOME WITH ME.

NO. I'M NOT.

DON'T BE SO STUBBORN!

IF YOU COME HOME AT ONCE, ALL WILL BE FORGIVEN.

I'LL TALK TO YOUR FATHER. YOU WON'T BE IN TROUBLE.

I WON'T GO WITH YOU, UNCLE.

I'VE ALREADY MADE MY VOWS TO GOD.

STOP THIS NONSENSE AT ONCE!!

BROTHER FRANCIS GAVE ME PERMISSION TO TAKE YOU HOME.

BROTHER FRANCIS TOLD ME YOU WHERE TO FIND YOU.

HE TOLD YOU BECAUSE HE KNOWS I WON'T GO.

THIS IS WHERE I BELONG.

I LOVE YOU AND I KNOW I CAN MAKE YOU HAPPY. MARRY ME AND YOU'LL NEVER REGRET IT.

YANK

I AM HAPPY, I AM GOD'S!

!!!!!

HER HAIR . . .

SHE CHOPPED IT ALL OFF!

CLARE! HOW COULD YOU?!

LET'S GO.

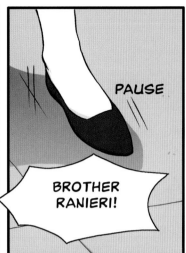

PAUSE

BROTHER RANIERI!

I WILL KEEP YOU IN MY PRAYERS. GOD BLESS YOU!

POOR LADIES
OF SAN DAMIANO

CLICK

FRANCIS ASKED CLARE TO LIVE AT THE CHURCH OF SAN DAMIANO.

SOON OTHER WOMEN JOINED HER. AMONG THEM WERE HER SISTER, CATERINA, WHO BECAME KNOWN AS AGNES; BONA; AND EVENTU-ALLY HER MOTHER, ORTOLANA, JOINED AFTER HER HUSBAND PASSED AWAY.

SISTER CLARE SPENT A LOT OF TIME IN PRAYER.

EVEN THOUGH HER ROLE WAS THE ABBESS, OR SPIRI-TUAL LEADER, CLARE WAS HUMBLE AND ALWAYS DID THE MOST DIFFICULT TASKS.

DID YOU REST WELL, SISTER BONA?

YES.

YOU ALWAYS WAKE UP BEFORE ME, SISTER CLARE!

WHEN DO YOU SLEEP, SISTER CLARE? YOU'RE THE LAST ONE TO GO TO BED AND THE FIRST TO WAKE UP.

YOU PRAY MORE THAN YOU SLEEP!

I'M FINE, SISTER BONA.

BEFORE WE WERE SISTERS, WE WERE FRIENDS, SISTER CLARE. I WORRY ABOUT YOU.

PLEASE DON'T WORRY. ALL IS WELL.

YOU NEED TO TAKE BETTER CARE OF YOURSELF.

I KNOW THAT AS ABBESS YOU PUT OUR NEEDS BEFORE YOUR OWN. BUT YOUR NEEDS ARE IMPORTANT TOO. THAT MEANS YOU NEED TO SLEEP WELL.

AGREED?

YOU'RE A GOOD FRIEND AND SISTER, BONA!

SIGH

I COULD SAY THE SAME ABOUT YOU!

IN ORDER TO SUPPORT THEMSELVES, THE SISTERS OFTEN WENT OUT TWO BY TWO TO BEG FOR WHAT THEY NEEDED.

SISTER CLARE!

SISTERS, HOW WAS YOUR DAY?

HESITATE

HESITATE

UM . . .

OK . . . WHAT'S GOING ON?

WE WERE BEGGING FOR FOOD IN THE VILLAGE, BUT WE DIDN'T GET MUCH.

!

SOME VILLAGERS YELLED HORRIBLE THINGS AT US! THEY THINK WOMEN SHOULDN'T BEG.

SPLASH

PLEASE, HAVE A SEAT.

SPLISH.

SPLOSH.

BROTHER FRANCIS OFTEN WENT TO A HERMITAGE* TO PRAY IN SOLITUDE. WHILE HE WAS THERE, SOMETIMES A FRIAR WOULD STOP TO SEE IF HE NEEDED ANYTHING.

PAT

*A SMALL HOUSE, HUT, OR SETTLEMENT FOR A RELIGIOUS PERSON TO LIVE AND PRAY ALONE WITH GOD.

I HOPE BROTHER FRANCIS' ILLNESS HASN'T GOTTEN ANY WORSE.

BROTHER FRANCIS?!

SURPRISE

!

STUMBLE

FRANCIS, YOU'RE STILL SICK. WHAT ARE YOU DOING OUT HERE?

ARE YOU LOOKING FOR SOMETHING?

BROTHER FRANCIS!?

WH–WHAT HAPPENED TO YOUR FACE?!

UGH . . . I'M FINE.

FINE?!

BROTHER LEO, YOU WORRY TOO MUCH.

BUT . . . UMM . . . I THINK I NEED YOUR HELP TO GET BACK.

OF COURSE.

STUMBLE

EVER SINCE BROTHER FRANCIS RETURNED FROM PREACHING IN THE CRUSADES HE HAS BEEN SO SICK. HIS EYES HURT CON-STANTLY AND HIS BODY GETS WEAKER AND WEAKER.

WHAT CAN I DO TO HELP HIM, LORD?

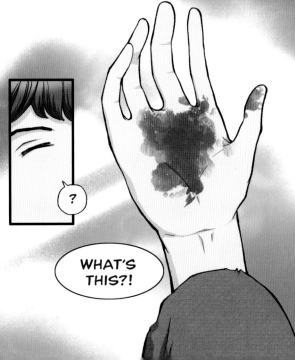

?

WHAT'S THIS?!

WHAT'S HAPPENING TO BROTHER FRANCIS!?

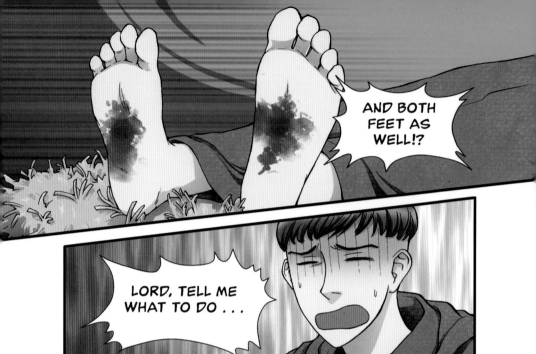

...

UMM...

OK, BROTHER FRANCIS...

BUT ONLY IF YOU LET ME TAKE CARE OF THOSE WOUNDS.

THANK YOU FOR UNDER-STANDING, BROTHER LEO.

I'LL BE BACK SOON!

TURN

SHAKE

TREMBLE

TREMBLE

MY GOD,
I LOVE YOU!

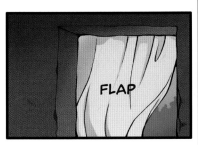

FLAP

RUSH

RUSH

NO NEED TO
HURRY, BROTHER
LEO.

I WANT TO
HELP YOU.

SPLISH

SPLOSH

BROTHER FRANCIS!

YOUR EYES ARE INFECTED AND YOU HAVE THE STIGMATA.

I'M WORRIED ABOUT YOUR HEALTH.

THE OTHER FRIARS ARE WORRIED, TOO.

CARDINAL UGOLINO WISHES YOU TO SEE A SPECIALIST IN RIETI. ON THE WAY WE CAN STOP AT SAN DAMIANO TO SEE THE SISTERS.

SAN DAMIANO?

YES, SISTER CLARE WOULD LIKE TO SEE YOU.

TIME THERE WOULD DO YOU GOOD.

BROTHER RUFINO TOLD ME THAT . . .

SISTER CLARE HAS BEEN VERY WORRIED ABOUT YOUR HEALTH.

. . .

SO PLEASE, LET ME TAKE YOU TO SAN DAMIANO AND THEN RIETI.

· · ·

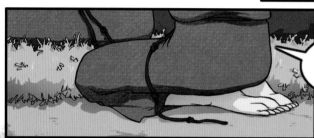

LET ME PRAY ABOUT IT.

IF WE GO, BROTHER FRANCIS, THE SISTERS WILL BE SO HAPPY. THEY WON'T WORRY AS MUCH.

AND MAYBE SISTER CLARE CAN GIVE ME SOME GOOD ADVICE.

WHILE AT SAN DAMIANO, BROTHER FRANCIS STAYED IN A LITTLE HERMITAGE NEXT TO THE CHAPLAIN'S HOUSE.

PACE ET BENE,* BROTHER FRANCIS.

IT'S ME, CLARE.

* PACE ET BENE MEANS PEACE AND GOOD. IT WAS THE TRADITIONAL GREETING USED BY FRANCIS AND HIS FOLLOWERS.

I WANT TO FEEL BROTHER WIND AND GREET SISTER EARTH.

SISTER CLARE.

YES, BROTHER FRANCIS?

I'M NOT SURE HOW MUCH LONGER I WILL BE IN THIS WORLD.

WHEN I'M GONE, PLEASE REMEMBER TO ALWAYS LOVE JESUS AND FOLLOW HIM IN HIS POVERTY.

PLEASE ASK ALL THE SISTERS . . .

. . .

TO EMBRACE THIS LIFE OF HOLY POVERTY AND TO LIVE IN CHRIST FOREVER.

AFTER FRANCIS DIED, CARDINAL UGOLINO BECAME POPE GREGORY IX. HE PROTECTED AND SUPPORTED THE YOUNG FRANCISCAN FAMILY. SISTER CLARE AND THE OTHER NUNS WERE KNOWN AS THE "ORDER OF POOR LADIES OF SAN DAMIANO." FRANCIS' BROTHERS BECAME THE "ORDER OF FRIARS MINOR."

WITH GOOD INTENTIONS, POPE GREGORY IX ENCOURAGED THE ORDER OF POOR LADIES TO OWN PROPERTY AND WANTED TO GIVE THEM GIFTS, BUT SISTER CLARE BELIEVED THIS WAS NOT IN KEEPING WITH FRANCIS' WISHES.

LADY CLARE, POPE GREGORY WOULD LIKE TO GIVE SOME POSSESSIONS AND PROPERTY TO THE SISTERS.

WILL YOU ACCEPT THEM?

NO.

WE MUST STAY TRUE TO GOD'S DESIRE FOR US TO LIVE POOR AS BROTHER FRANCIS TAUGHT!

I DON'T UNDERSTAND WHY POPE GREGORY IS DOING THIS.

I'M SURE THE HOLY FATHER THINKS HE IS ACTING IN OUR BEST INTEREST,

BUT HE HAS FORGOTTEN THAT WE TOOK A VOW OF POVERTY!

EVEN WHEN BROTHER FRANCIS WAS ALIVE, THERE WERE MANY OBJECTIONS TO SEEING THE SISTERS BEG.

JESUS, MANY OF THE SISTERS IN OUR OTHER CONVENTS HAVE TURNED FROM THE WAY OF POVERTY. BUT I BELIEVE THAT YOU WANT US TO CONTINUE AS WE ALWAYS HAVE.

HELP US TO REMAIN FAITHFUL, TO LIVE AS YOU DID.

I'M WORRIED THAT WHEN I DIE THE SISTERS HERE IN SAN DAMIANO WILL QUIT PRACTICING OUR WAY OF STRICT POVERTY. WHAT SHOULD I DO, LORD?

SISTER CLARE PRAYED AND PRAYED UNTIL SHE WAS CERTAIN HOW THE LORD WANTED HER TO PROCEED.

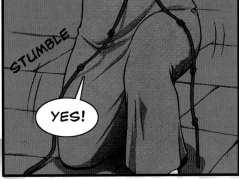

STUMBLE

YES!

I WILL WRITE A NEW SET OF RULES FOR THE ORDER OF POOR LADIES.

JESUS WAS A POOR TRAVELING PREACHER WHO OWNED NOTHING.

GRIP

AND WE ARE CALLED TO LIVE JUST LIKE OUR LORD.

GOD HAS INVITED US TO THIS LIFE AND WE HAVE ACCEPTED!

IT WON'T BE EASY TO GET APPROVAL FOR OUR NEW RULES. BUT I MUST TRY!

RULE TO LIVE BY

SAN DAMIANO, 1252

GOOD TO SEE YOU CARDINAL RAYNALDUS.*

IT'S GOOD TO SEE YOU, SISTER AGNES.

THANK YOU FOR COMING. SISTER CLARE HAS SOMETHING TO ASK YOU.

NOD

I HEARD THAT YOU HAD OPENED A CONVENT IN MONTICELLI. YOU'RE BACK?

I CAME BECAUSE I WAS WORRIED ABOUT CLARE.

I SEE.

*CARDINAL RAYNALDUS WAS THE CARDINAL PROTECTOR OF THE POOR LADIES OF ASSISI. THIS MEANT THAT HE DEFENDED AND ACTED IN THEIR BEST INTEREST.

HOW IS SISTER CLARE'S HEALTH?

SHE'S NOT WELL.

BUT YOU KNOW SISTER CLARE, EVEN THOUGH SHE'S SICK IN BED . . .

SHE INSISTS THAT SHE CAN WORK. SHE ALSO NEVER MISSES OUR TIMES OF PRAYER.

OF COURSE!

KNOCK

JUST LIKE BROTHER FRANCIS, SHE WON'T SLOW DOWN.

KNOCK

KNOCK

SISTER CLARE, THE CARDINAL IS HERE.

PLOP

*FROM THE EIGHTH CENTURY UNTIL THE MID-NINETEENTH CENTURY A LARGE PART OF ITALY WAS UNDER THE DIRECT RULE OF THE POPE. EMPEROR FREDERICK WAGED WAR AGAINST THE POPE FOR CONTROL OF THE PAPAL STATES IN UMBRIA.

FLASHBACK TO
SEPTEMBER 1240

HUM DE
DUM

WHISTLE

VIBRATIONS!!

?

* NOMADS FROM THE SYRIAN AND ARABIAN DESERT KNOWN FOR THEIR CALVARY. THEY FOUGHT ON EMPEROR FREDERICK'S SIDE DURING THE WAR.

MAYBE HE IS RETALIATING BECAUSE THE POPE EXCOMMUNICATED HIM!

I STILL CAN'T UNDERSTAND WHY HE WOULD JOIN FORCES WITH THE SARACENS . . .

AND ATTACK THE INNOCENT PEOPLE OF UMBRIA!

WE CAN'T GIVE IN TO HIS SCARE TACTICS!!

ATTACK!!

SIR, A MONASTERY!

!

GO!!

THEY'RE PROBABLY LOYAL TO THE POPE! KILL THEM ALL!

WOO

YES!

CLIP CLOP CLIP CLOP

I CAN HEAR THE SOLDIERS' HORSES COMING CLOSER!

!!!

WHAT SHOULD WE DO?

GATHER THE SISTERS OUTSIDE THE CHAPEL AT ONCE!

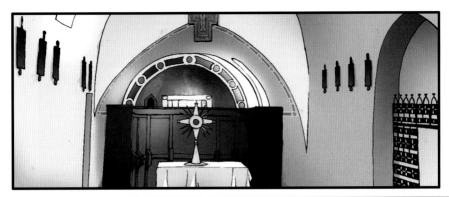

MY DEAR SISTERS, WE MUST TRUST IN GOD.

SHAKE, TREMBLE, SHAKE

IN THE BIBLE, JESUS TELLS HIS FOLLOWERS TO NOT BE AFRAID.

GOD IS WITH US, SISTERS. NO ONE WILL HURT US.

BUT SISTER CLARE . . .

LET'S PRAY AND ENTRUST OUR SAFETY TO GOD.

DRAG EVERYONE OUT AND KILL THEM ALL!

SHOW NO MERCY!

!

FILLED WITH CONFIDENCE THAT GOD WOULD KEEP THEM SAFE, CLARE WENT TO THE CHAPEL.

!

WHEN SHE CAME OUT SHE WAS HOLDING A MONSTRANCE* CONTAINING JESUS IN THE BLESSED SACRAMENT.

*A SACRED VESSEL THAT HOLDS THE BLESSED SACRAMENT FOR TIMES OF PUBLIC ADORATION.

?

BE GONE! YOU MAY NOT ENTER THIS HOLY PLACE!

DON'T JUST STAND THERE! SHE'S NOTHING BUT A WEAK WOMAN!

WE ARE UNDER THE LORD JESUS' PROTECTION. YOU MAY NOT ENTER HERE!!

NON . . .

. . . SENSE?

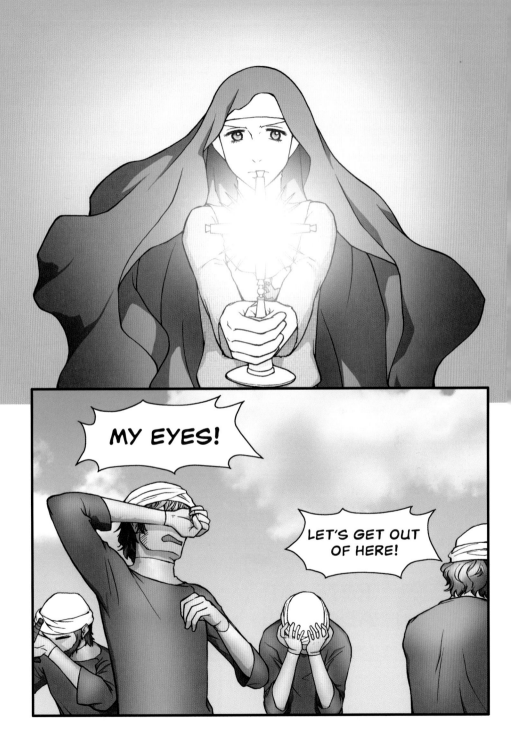

DARN IT!

RETREAT!!

RETREAT AT ONCE!!

SHAKE

SHAKE

KNEEL

JESUS . . .

THANK YOU . . .

IT'S HARD TO BELIEVE THAT ALL HAPPENED JUST TWELVE YEARS AGO.

JESUS...

YOU WERE SO BRAVE.

CARDINAL RAYNALDUS,

I ASKED YOU TO COME SO THAT...

YOU COULD HELP US GET THE POPE'S APPROVAL FOR THE RULE I HAVE WRITTEN FOR OUR ORDER.

UMMM...

YOU SERVE AS OUR CARDINAL PROTECTOR, RIGHT?

SISTER CLARE, WHAT YOU WANT IS JUST TOO DIFFICULT. THERE HAS NEVER BEEN AN ORDER OF WOMEN LIVING THE WAY YOU WANT TO LIVE.

AND AS YOU KNOW,

NOT SO LONG AGO POPE INNOCENT CALLED THE FOURTH LATERAN COUNCIL.

ONE OF THE RESULTS OF THAT COUNCIL IS THE DECISION THAT NEW RELIGIOUS ORDERS, SUCH AS YOURS, MUST ADOPT ALREADY ESTABLISHED RULES. THERE CAN BE NO NEW RULES.

YOUR RULE JUST WOULDN'T BE APPROVED.

BUT, CARDINAL RAYNALDUS . . .

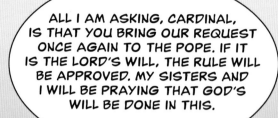

I AM DOING WHAT I BELIEVE GOD HAS ASKED OF ME.

WHAT GREAT FAITH SHE HAS! DEAR GOD, HELP ME TO HELP THIS HOLY WOMAN!

AUGUST 1253

SISTER CLARE HAS HARDLY EATEN ANYTHING FOR TWO WEEKS.

SHE IS SO THIN AND WEAK.

SHE CAN'T GET OUT OF BED WITHOUT HELP.

SHE KEEPS SAYING THAT SHE IS FINE AND THAT I SHOULDN'T WORRY.

BUT I KNOW SHE IS WAITING FOR POPE INNOCENT IV TO APPROVE THE RULE SHE WROTE.

IT WOULD MEAN SO MUCH TO HER.

WELL, AT LEAST YOU KNOW THAT YOU HAVE THE FULL SUPPORT OF CARDINAL RAYNALDUS.

I BELIEVE THAT SOME DAY THE POPE WILL APPROVE THE RULE AS WELL.

BUT I . . .

WONDER IF IT WILL HAPPEN BEFORE . . .

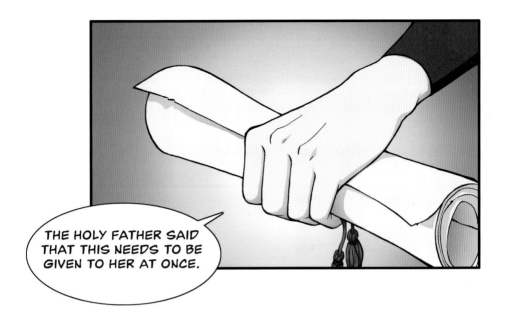

THE HOLY FATHER SAID THAT THIS NEEDS TO BE GIVEN TO HER AT ONCE.

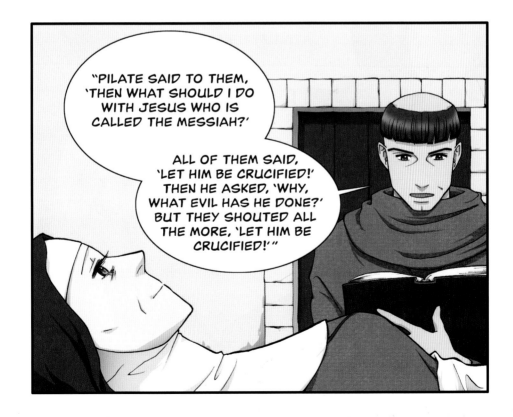

"PILATE SAID TO THEM, 'THEN WHAT SHOULD I DO WITH JESUS WHO IS CALLED THE MESSIAH?'

ALL OF THEM SAID, 'LET HIM BE CRUCIFIED!' THEN HE ASKED, 'WHY, WHAT EVIL HAS HE DONE?' BUT THEY SHOUTED ALL THE MORE, 'LET HIM BE CRUCIFIED!'"

PLEASE HELP ME SIT UP, BROTHER JUNIPERO.

OF COURSE.

UMPH!

MAY I SEE THE LETTER, SISTER?

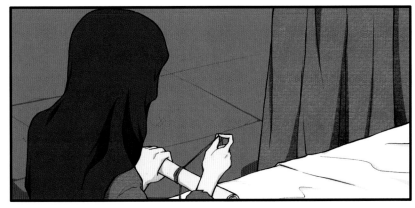

TREMBLE

SHAKE

AT LONG LAST POPE INNOCENT IV HAD APPROVED THE RULE SISTER CLARE HAD WRITTEN! DESPITE HER WEAKNESS, CLARE AND HER SISTERS WERE FILLED WITH JOY. NOW THE POOR LADIES OF ASSISI COULD LIVE THE LIFE OF POVERTY TO WHICH THE LORD HAD CALLED THEM.

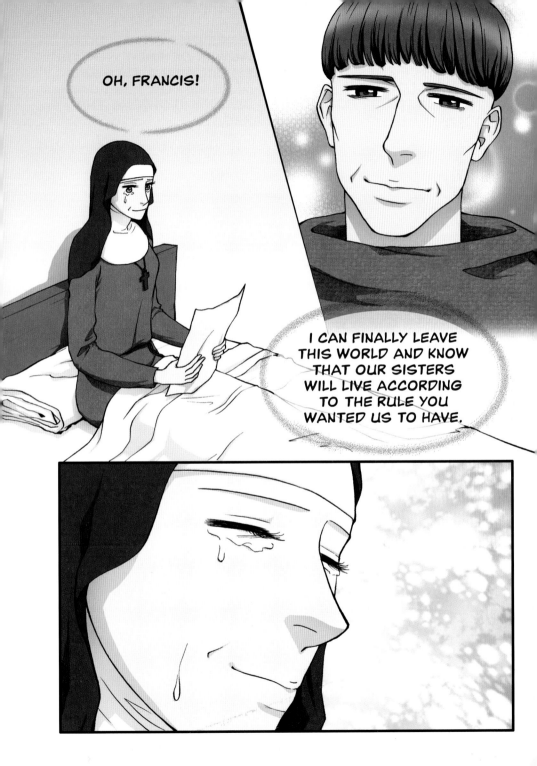

THE NEXT DAY—ON AUGUST II—CLARE DIED PEACEFULLY. SHE WAS THE FIRST FEMALE FOLLOWER OF SAINT FRANCIS AND THE FIRST WOMAN TO GET APPROVED A RULE SHE HAD WRITTEN FOR A RELIGIOUS ORDER. AFTER HER DEATH, THE ORDER OF POOR LADIES BECAME KNOWN AS THE "POOR CLARES."

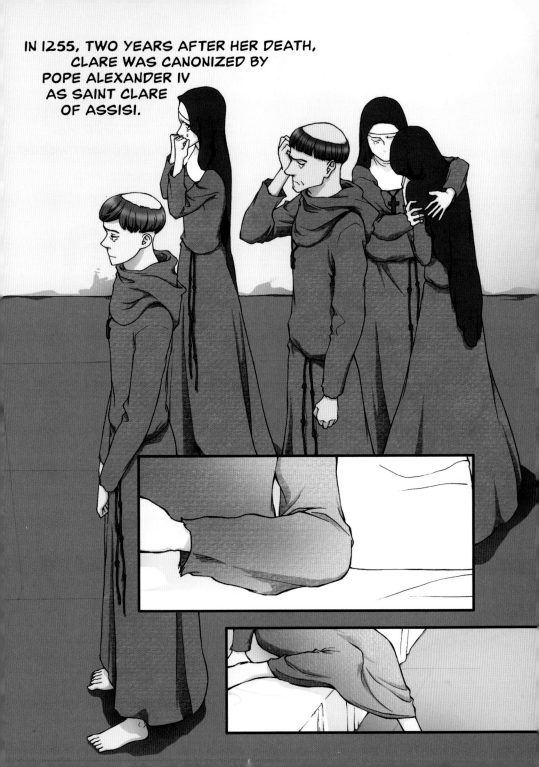

IN 1255, TWO YEARS AFTER HER DEATH, CLARE WAS CANONIZED BY POPE ALEXANDER IV AS SAINT CLARE OF ASSISI.

"BLESSED BE YOU, O MY GOD, FOR HAVING CREATED ME."

SAINT CLARE'S LAST WORDS

Courage

Pauline .KIDS

Commitment

Compassion

These are just some of the qualities of the saints you'll find in our popular Encounter the Saints series. Join Saint John Neumann, Saint Clare of Assisi, Saint Francis of Assisi, and many other holy men and women as they discover and try to do what God asks of them. Get swept into the exciting and inspiring lives of the Church's heroes and heroines while encountering the saints in a new and fun way!

Collect all the
Encounter the Saints books
by visiting
www.paulinestore.com/
EncountertheSaints

ENCOUNTER THE SAINTS SERIES

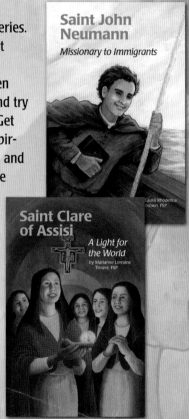

Saint John Neumann

Missionary to Immigrants

Laura Rhoderica Brown, FSP

Saint Clare of Assisi

A Light for the World

by Marianne Lorraine Trouvé, FSP

Saint Francis of Assisi

Gentle Revolutionary

by Mary Emmanuel Alves, FSP

Prayers for Young Catholics

is a book of basic and more advanced prayers. Beautifully expressed through artwork, it explains the importance of prayer and provides instruction on how to pray.

For young Catholics ages 8–12.

For My Friends

Jesus, you gave me the gift of my friends. Their friendship and love remind me of your love and faithfulness. Thank you for my friends. Help me to be a good friend to each of them. Teach me to be someone who listens, serves, and loves. Let all of my friendships be modeled on my relationship ...
to remember ...
Amen.

For All Children

Jesus, you said, "Let the little children come to me." I pray for all children of the world: for those in my school, in my town, ... but also for those in all ...

Dear and Sweet Mother Mary

Dear and sweet Mother Mary, keep your holy hand upon me; guard my mind, my heart, and my senses, that I may never commit sin. Sanctify my thoughts, affections, words, and actions, so that I may please you and your Jesus, my God, and ...

Hail, Holy Queen

Hail, holy Queen, Mother of Mercy, our life, our sweetness, and our hope. To you do we cry, poor banished children of Eve; to you do we send up our sighs, mourning and weeping in this valley of tears. Turn then, most gracious advocate, your eyes of mercy toward us, and after this our exile, show unto us the blessed fruit of your womb, Jesus. O clement, O loving, O sweet Virgin Mary.

OUR
CATHOLIC
FAITH

PRAYERS
FOR
Young
CATHOLICS

PRAYERS
TO MARY

Features & Benefits:

- Offers a presentation page for gift givers

- Contains original prayers that are reflective of children's needs

- Ideal gift for young Catholics, 1st Communion, birthdays, and more

ISBN: 0-8198-5995-8 $14.95

Fabulous Faith Stories

**Fantastic stories
that show kids
how to live their
faith!**

For more information about
these and other great titles
for kids of all ages go to
www.paulinestore.com

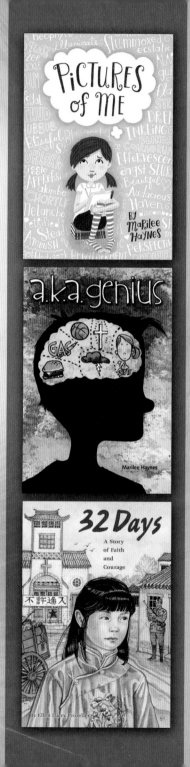

Who are the Daughters of St. Paul?

We are Catholic sisters with a mission. Our task is to bring the love of Jesus to everyone like Saint Paul did. You can find us in over 50 countries. Our founder, Blessed James Alberione, showed us how to reach out to the world through the media. That's why we publish books, make movies and apps, record music, broadcast on radio, perform concerts, help people at our bookstores, visit parishes, host JClub book fairs, use social media and the Internet, and pray for all of you.

Visit our Web site at www.pauline.org

Pauline
BOOKS & MEDIA

The Daughters of St. Paul operate book and media centers at the following addresses. Visit, call, or write the one nearest you today, or find us at www.paulinestore.org.

CALIFORNIA
3908 Sepulveda Blvd, Culver City, CA 90230   310-397-8676
3250 Middlefield Road, Menlo Park, CA 94025   650-369-4230

FLORIDA
145 SW 107th Avenue, Miami, FL 33174   305-559-6715

HAWAII
1143 Bishop Street, Honolulu, HI 96813   808-521-2731

ILLINOIS
172 North Michigan Avenue, Chicago, IL 60601   312-346-4228

LOUISIANA
4403 Veterans Memorial Blvd, Metairie, LA 70006   504-887-7631

MASSACHUSETTS
885 Providence Hwy, Dedham, MA 02026   781-326-5385

MISSOURI
9804 Watson Road, St. Louis, MO 63126   314-965-3512

NEW YORK
64 West 38th Street, New York, NY 10018   212-754-1110

SOUTH CAROLINA
243 King Street, Charleston, SC 29401   843-577-0175

TEXAS—Currently no book center; for parish exhibits or outreach evangelization, contact: 210-569-0500 or SanAntonio@paulinemedia.com or P.O. Box 761416, San Antonio, TX 78245

VIRGINIA
1025 King Street, Alexandria, VA 22314   703-549-3806

CANADA
3022 Dufferin Street, Toronto, ON M6B 3T5   416-781-9131

SMILE God loves you